Dimetrodon
Apatosaurus

Procompsognathus

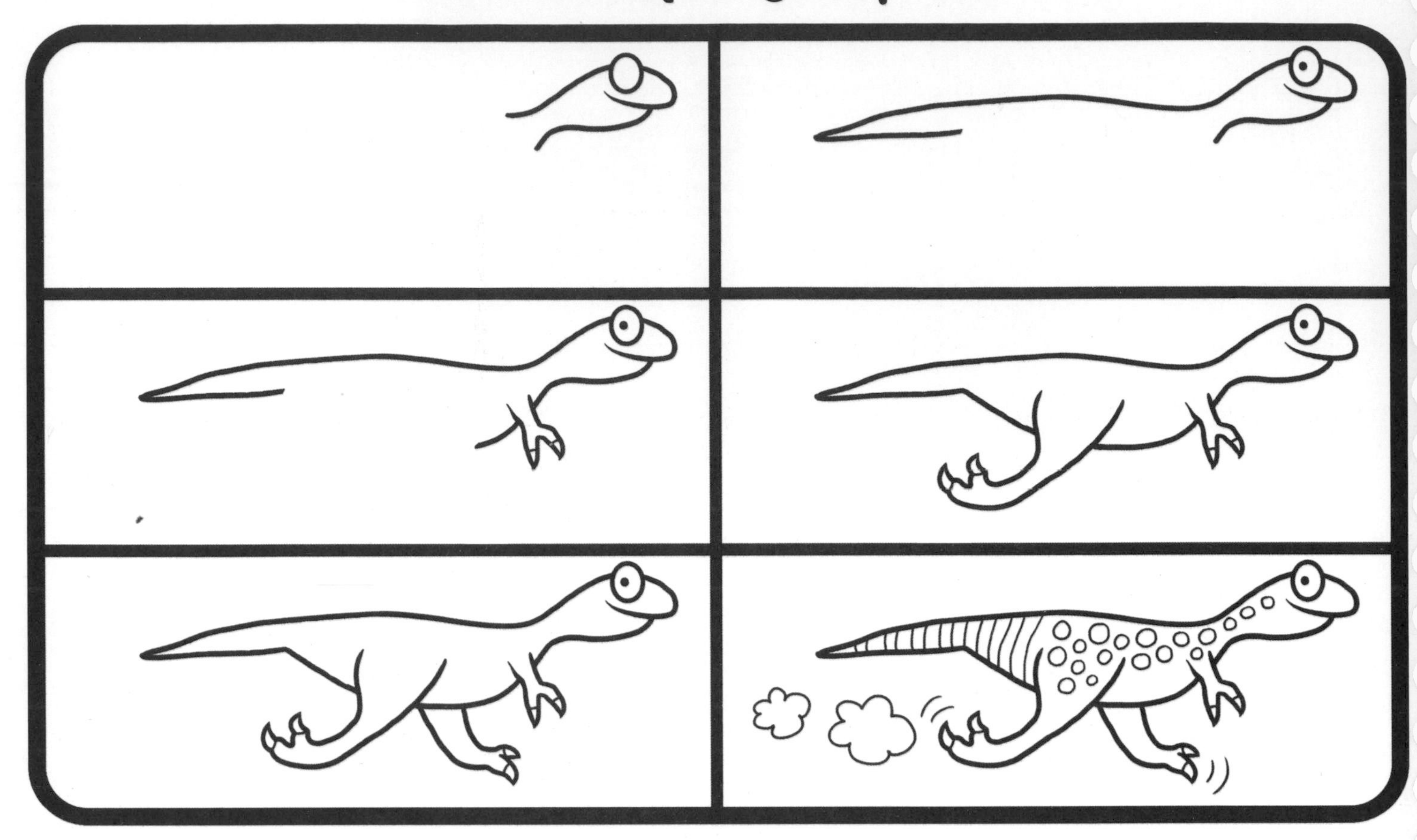

Pterodactyl

Ankylosaurus

Goyocephale

Isanosaurus
Ceratosaurus

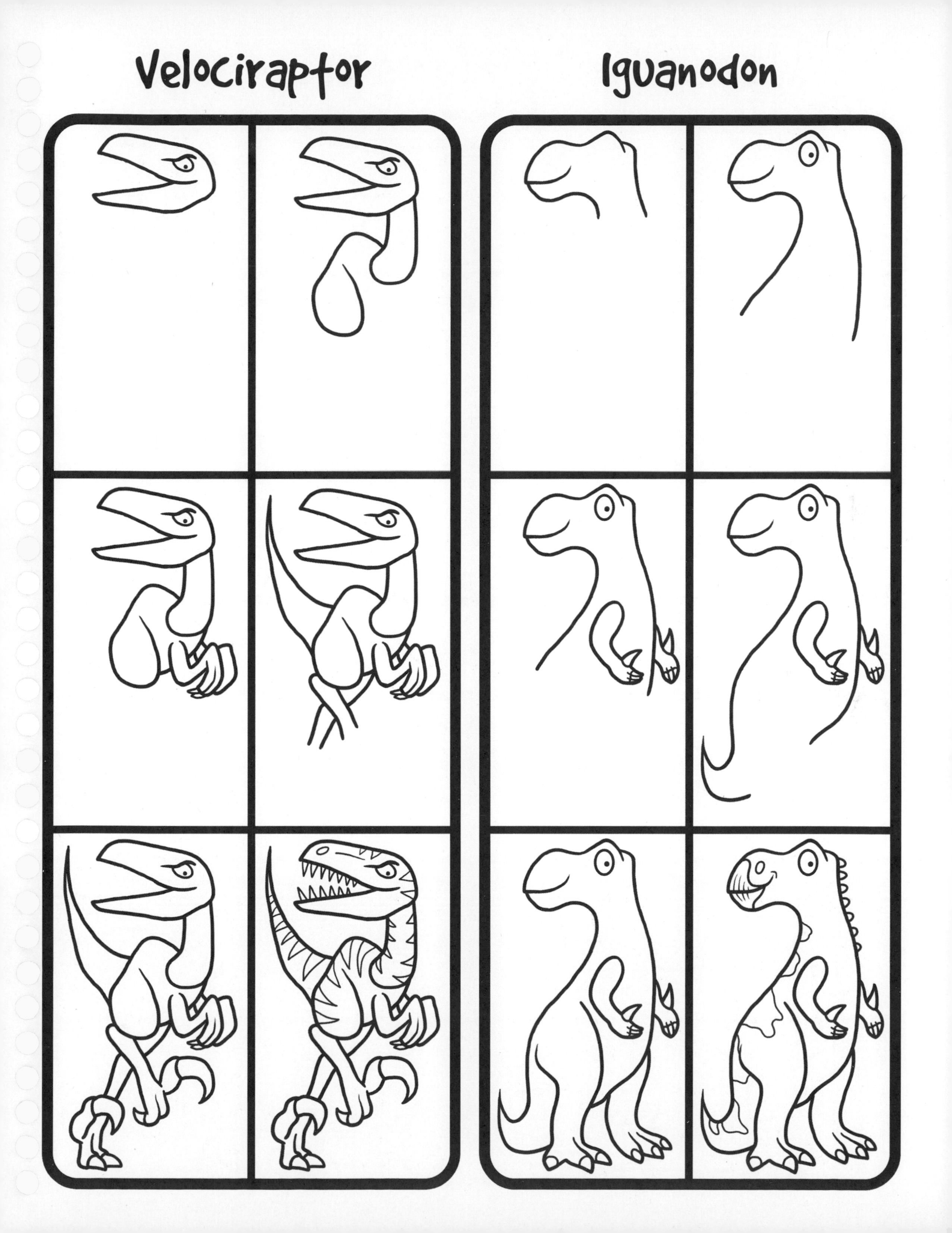
Velociraptor
Iguanodon

Diplodocus

Vulcanodon

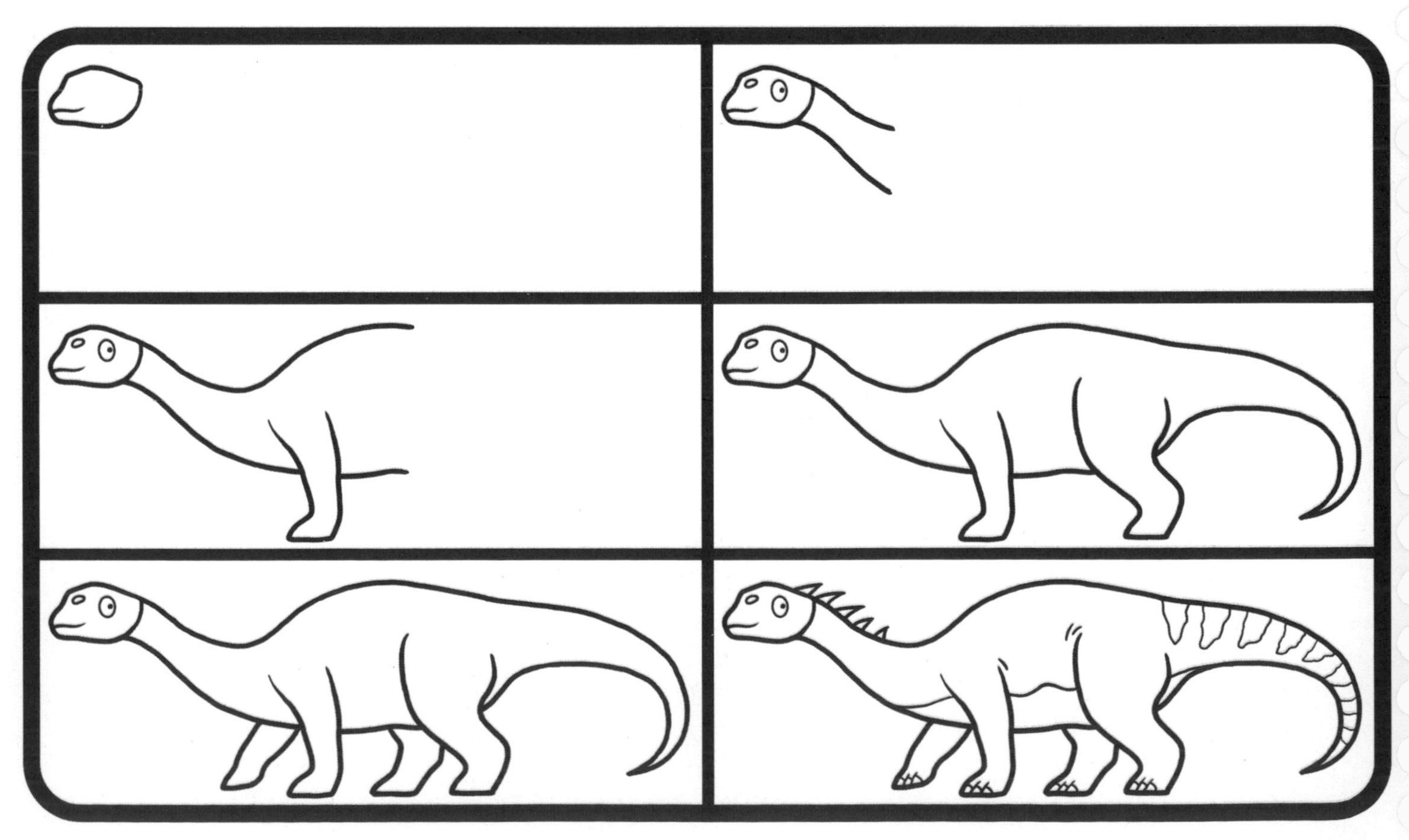

Brachiosaurus

Stegosaurus

Amargasaurus

Antarctosaurus

Omeisaurus
Triceratops

coelophysis

ornitholestes

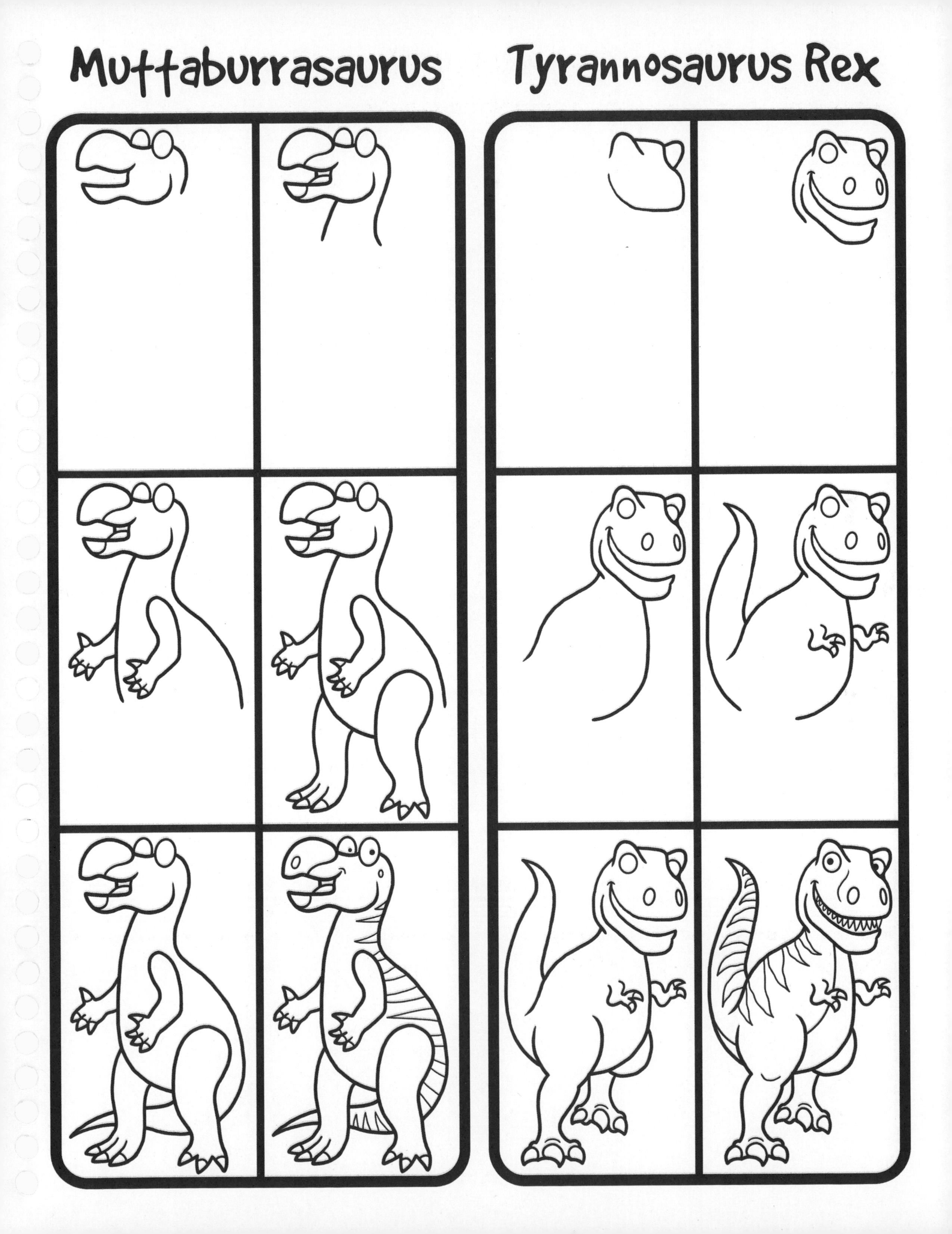
Muttaburrasaurus
Tyrannosaurus Rex

Pachycephalosaurus
Parasaurolophus

Troodon
Corythosaurus

Elaphrosaurus

Hoplitosaurus

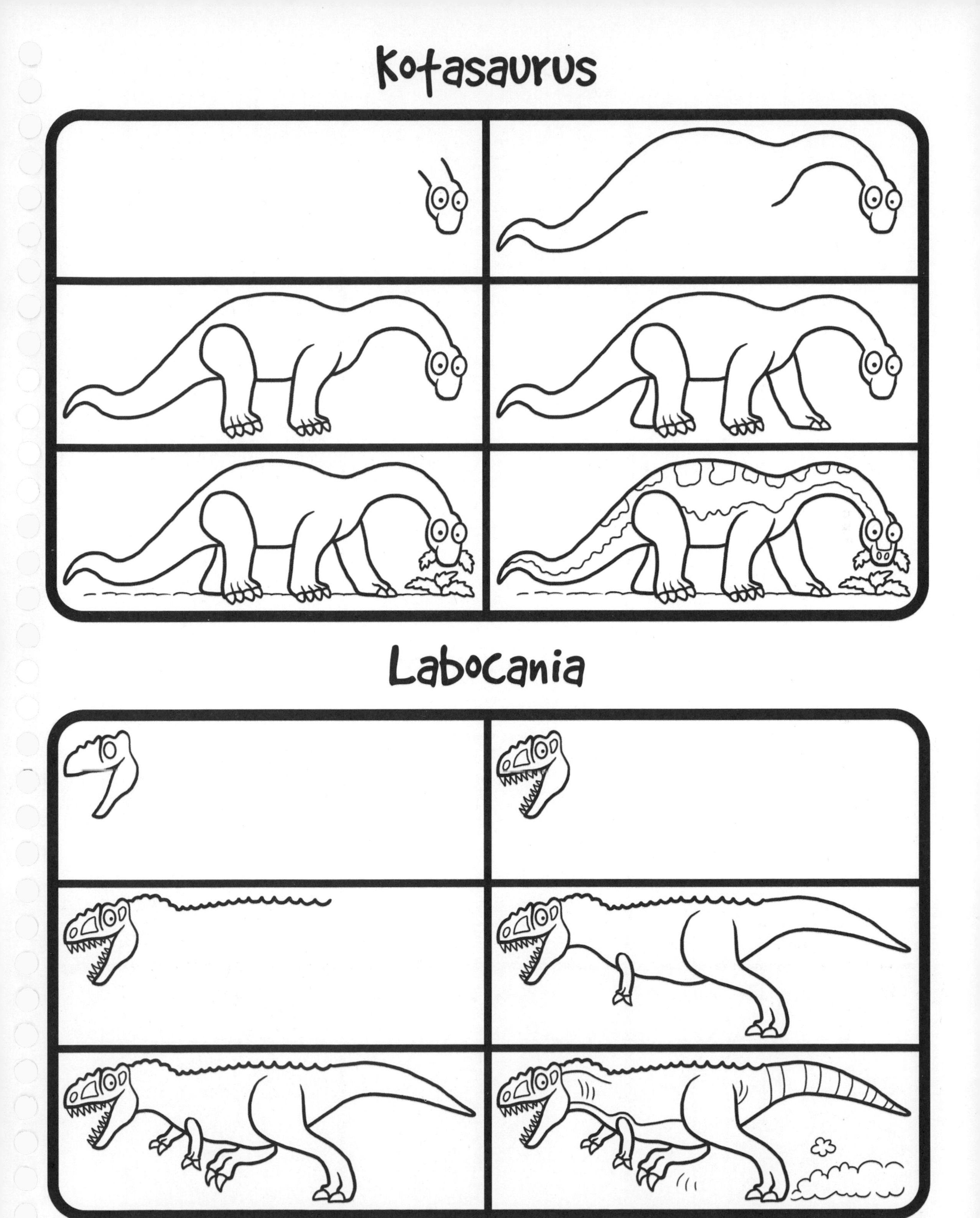
Kotasaurus
Labocania

Baryonyx

Carnotaurus

Chasmosaurus

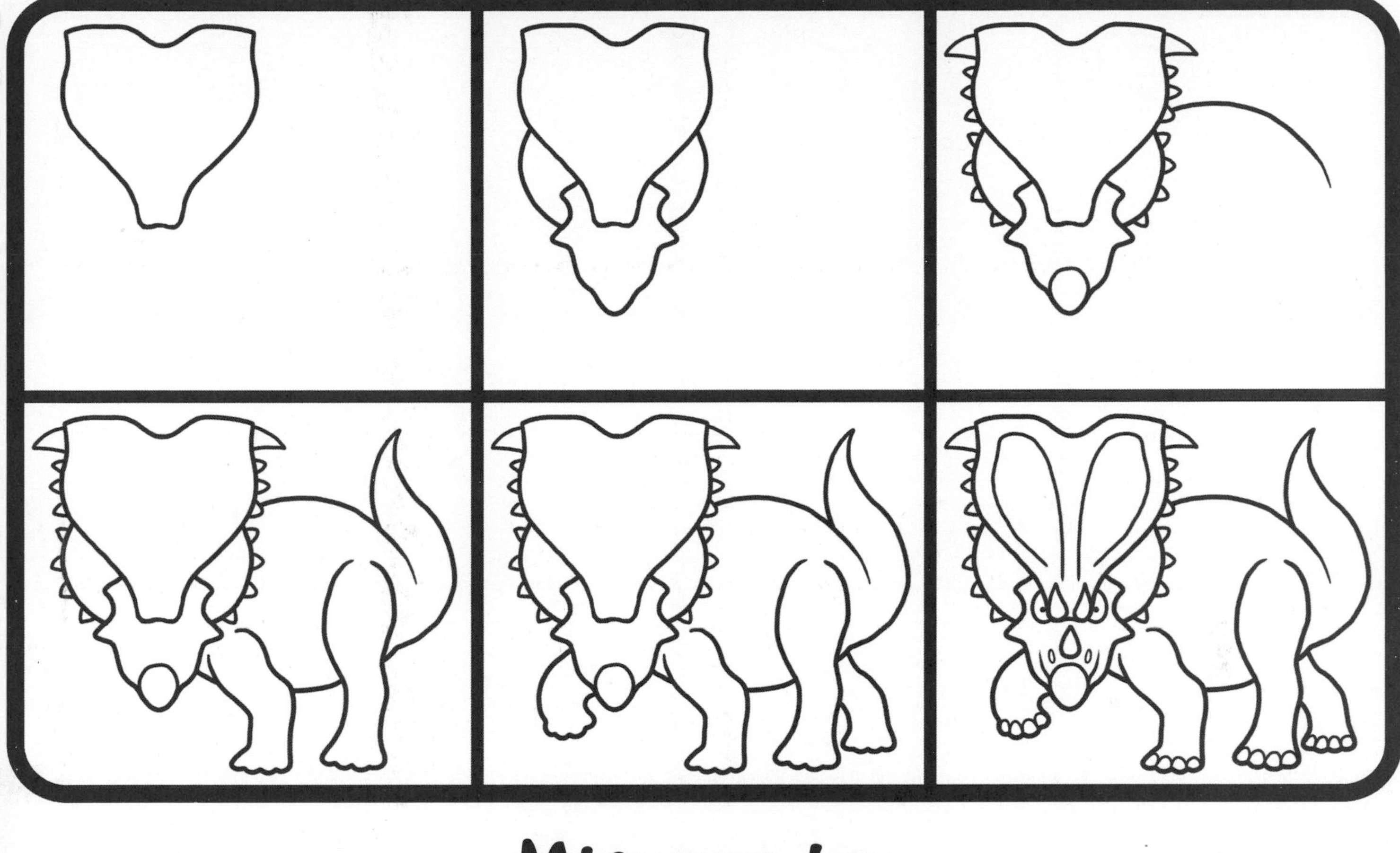

Microraptor

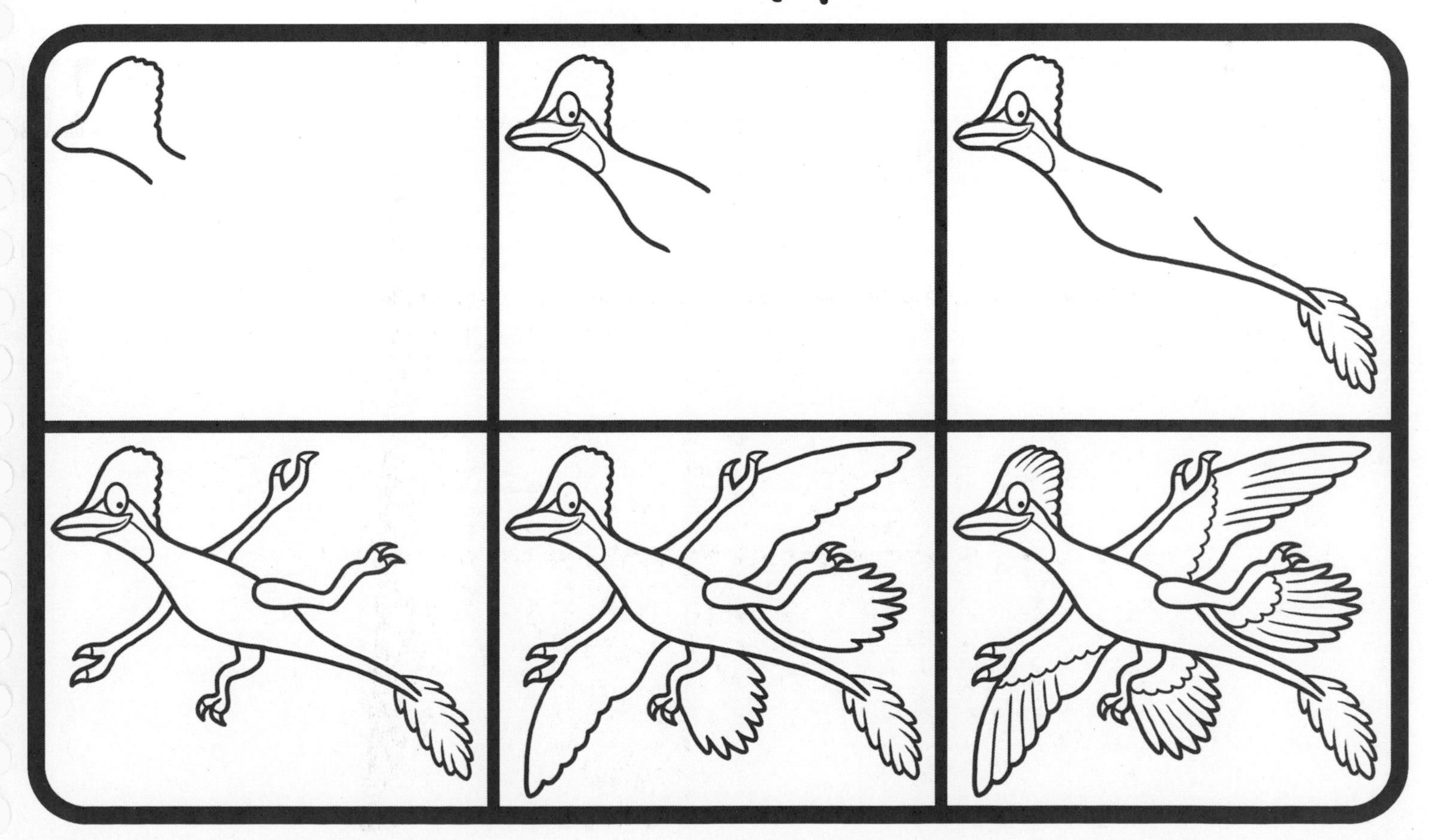

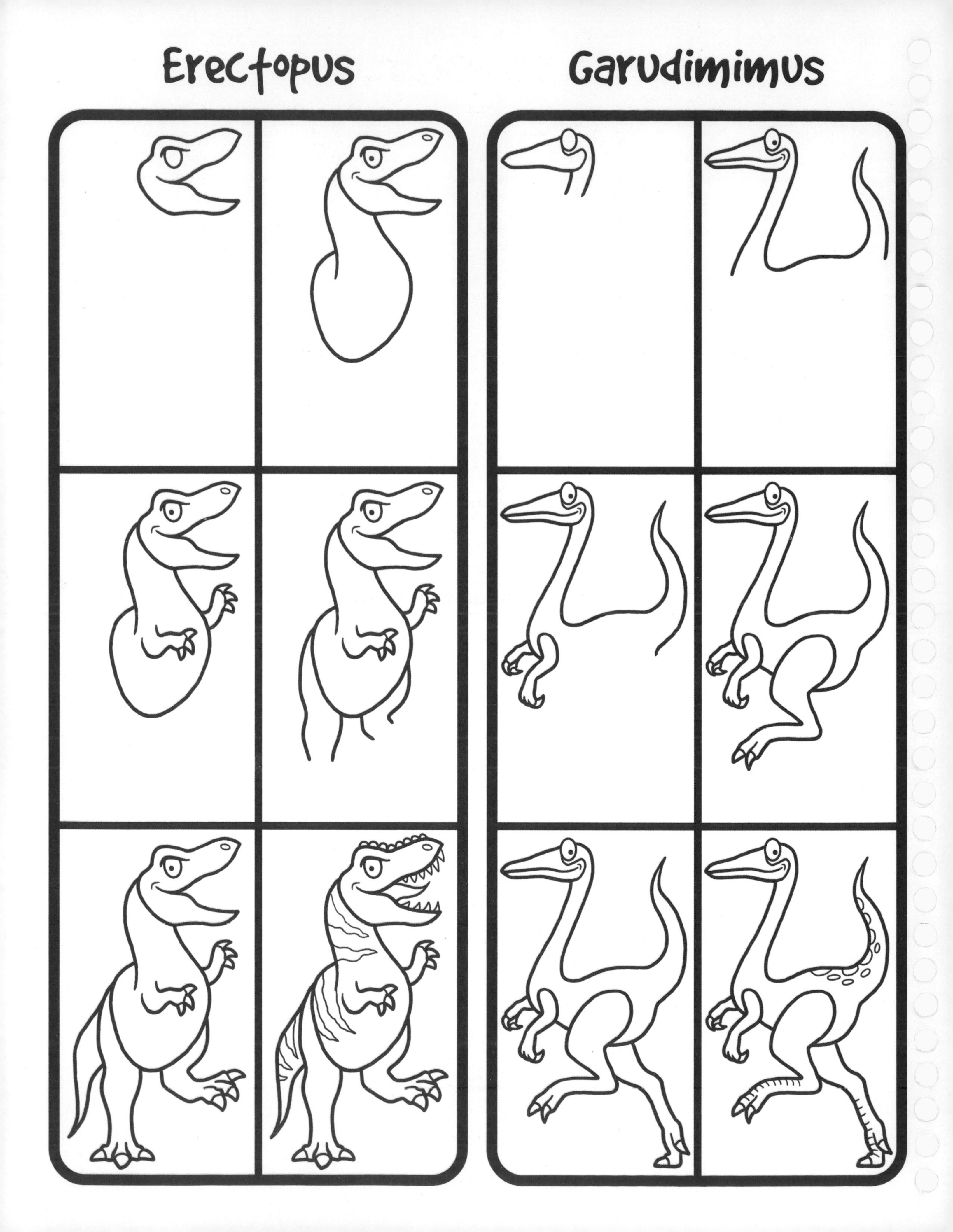
Erectopus
Garudimimus

Indosaurus

Ingenia

Malawisaurus

Mongolosaurus

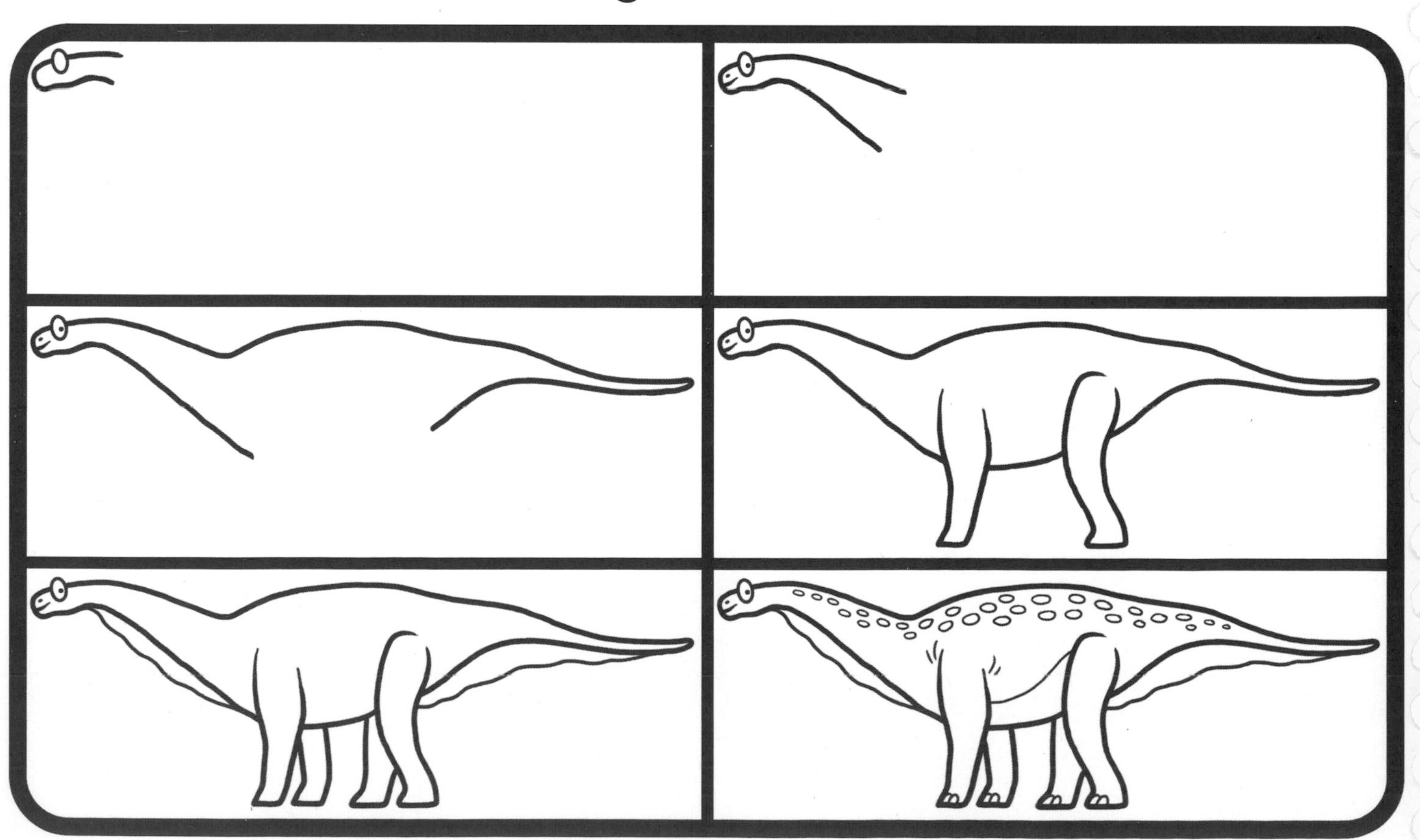

Nemegtosaurus

Nipponosaurus

Deinonychus

Gallimimus

Ouranosaurus

Liopleurodon

Jaxartosaurus
Lambeosaurus

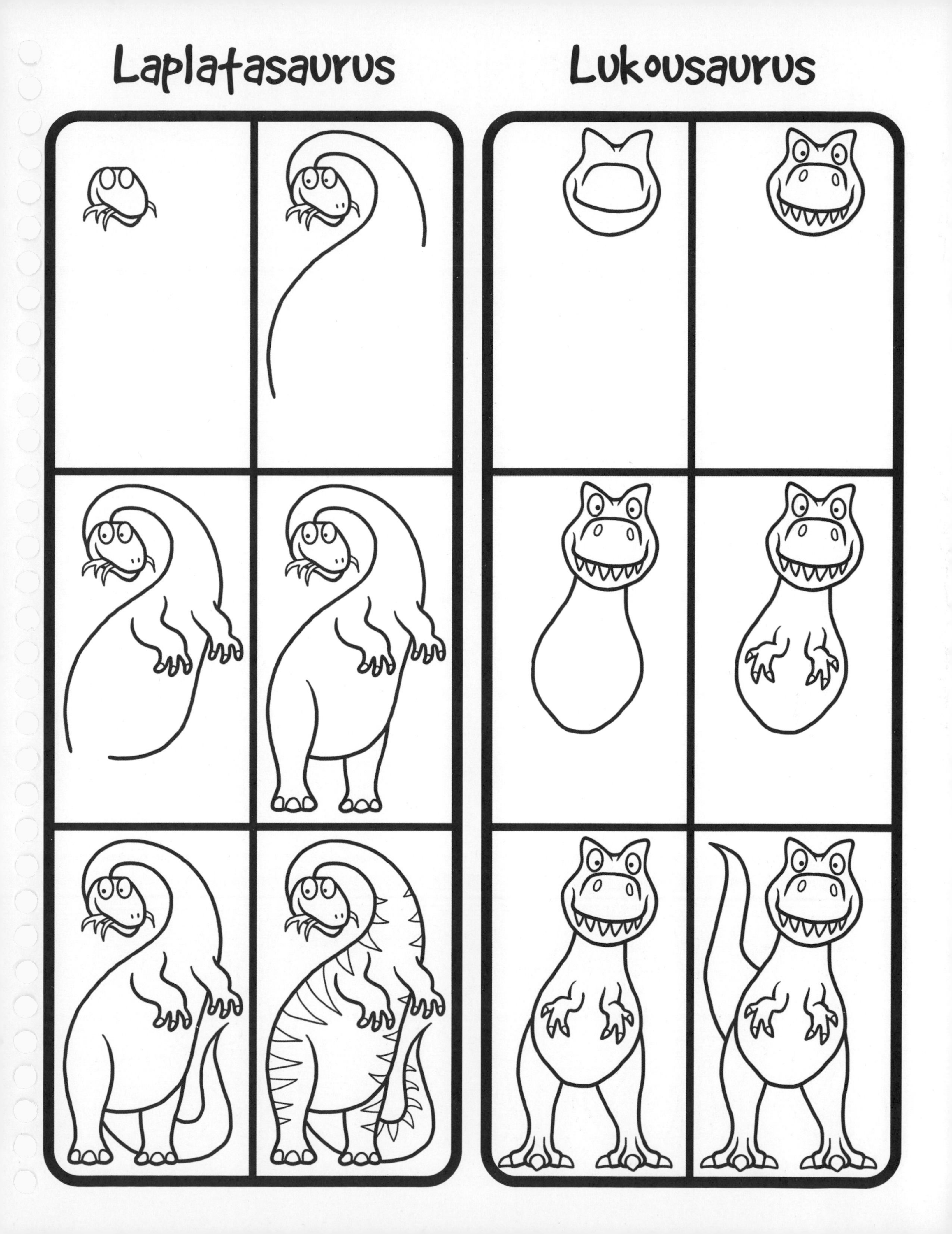
Laplatasaurus
Lukousaurus

Neuquensaurus

Orodromeus

Patagosaurus

Supersaurus

Protoceratops

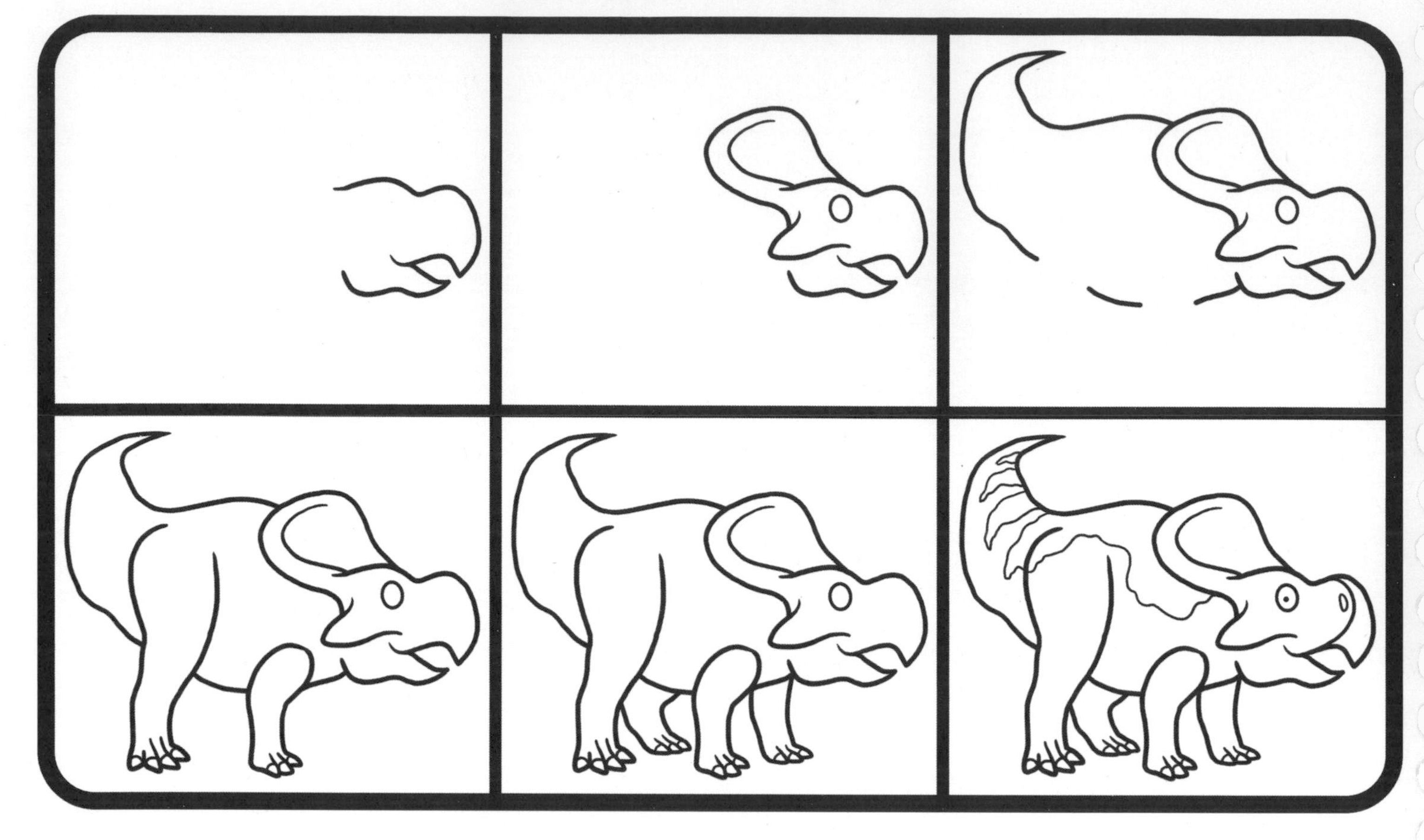

Psittacosaurus

Spinosaurus

Archaeopteryx

Tarbosaurus
Mononykus

Lophostropheus
Sarcolestes

Titanosaurus

Quetzalcoatlus

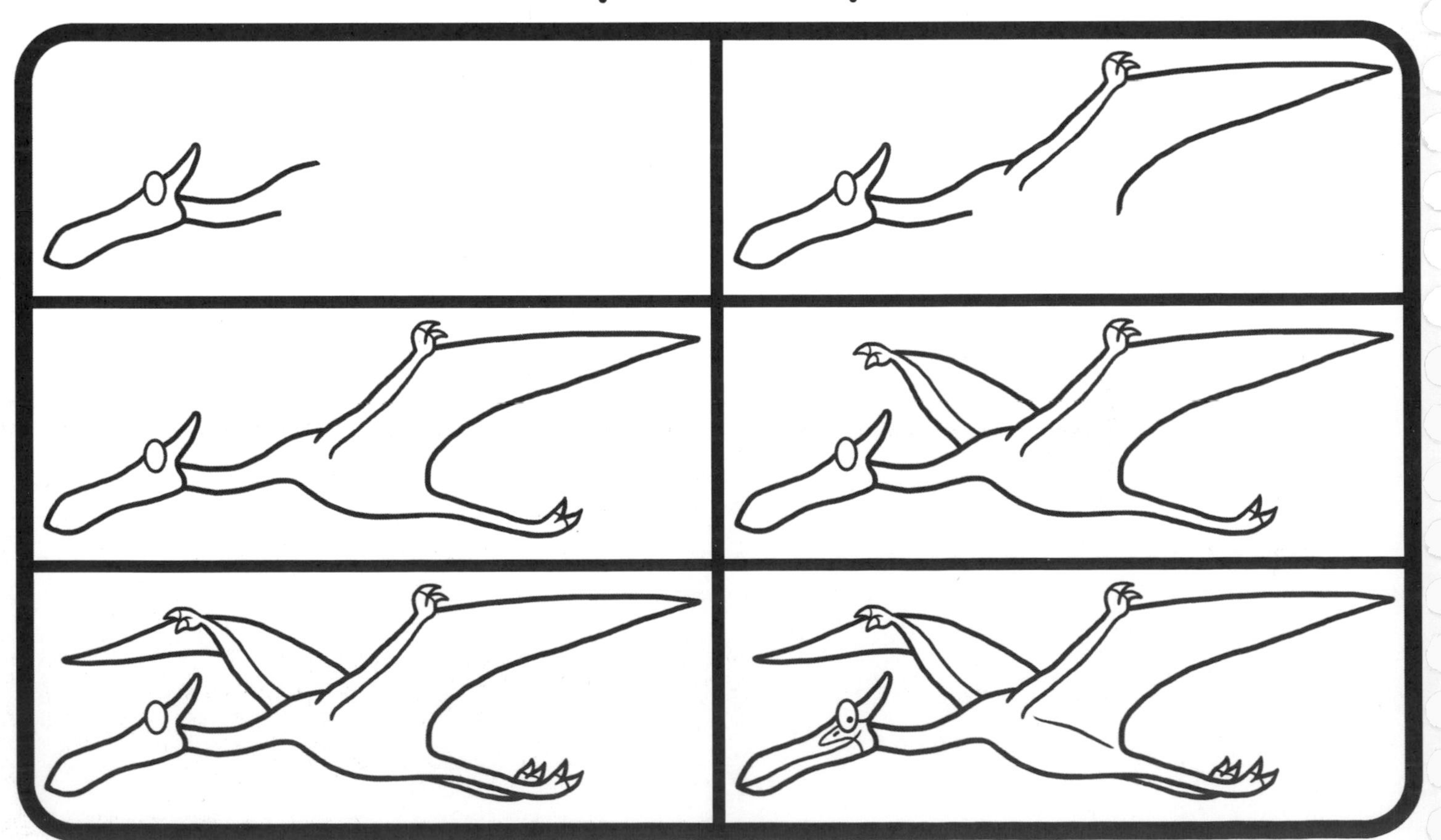

Peteinosaurus

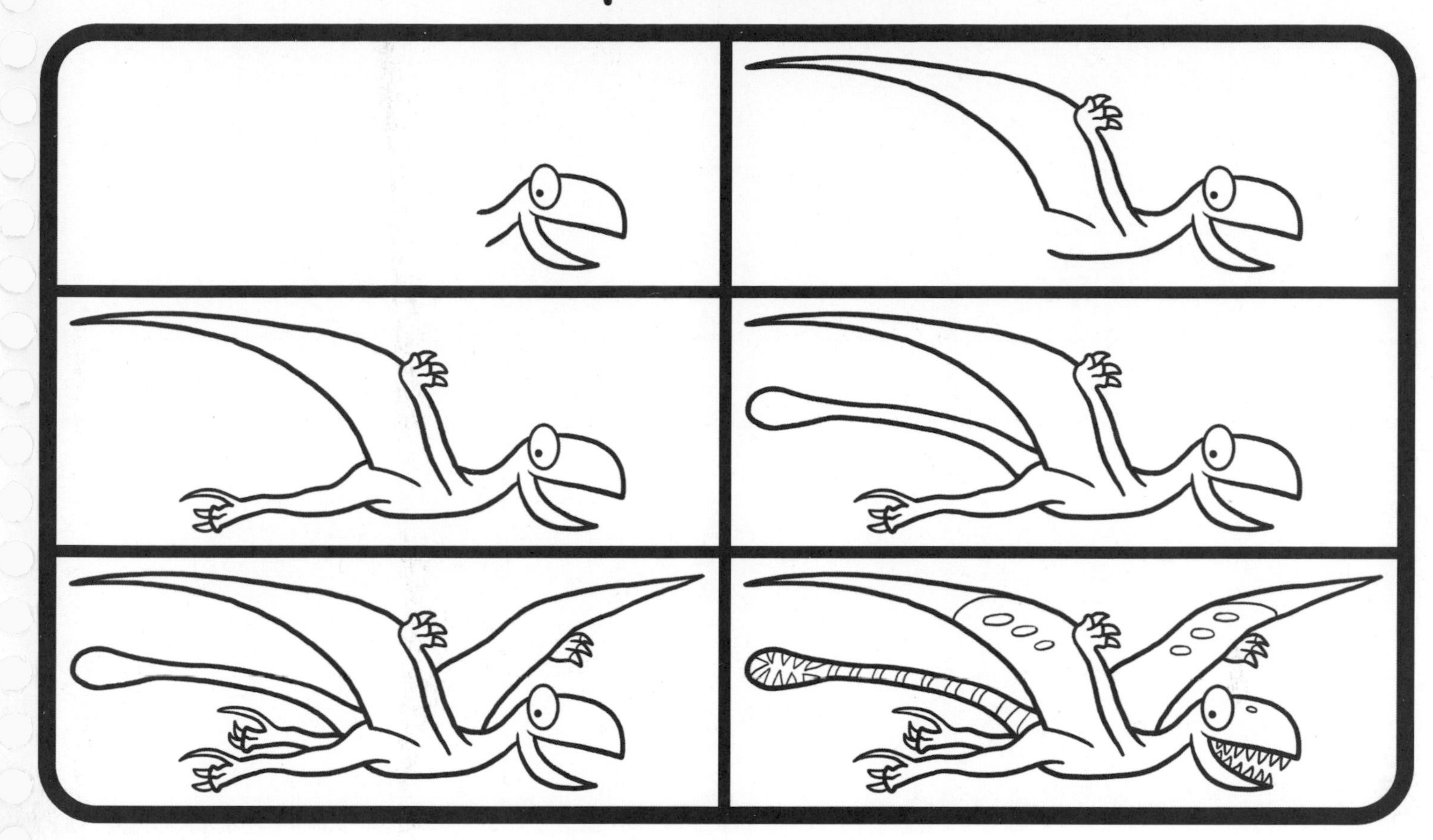

Mussaurus

Kentrosaurus

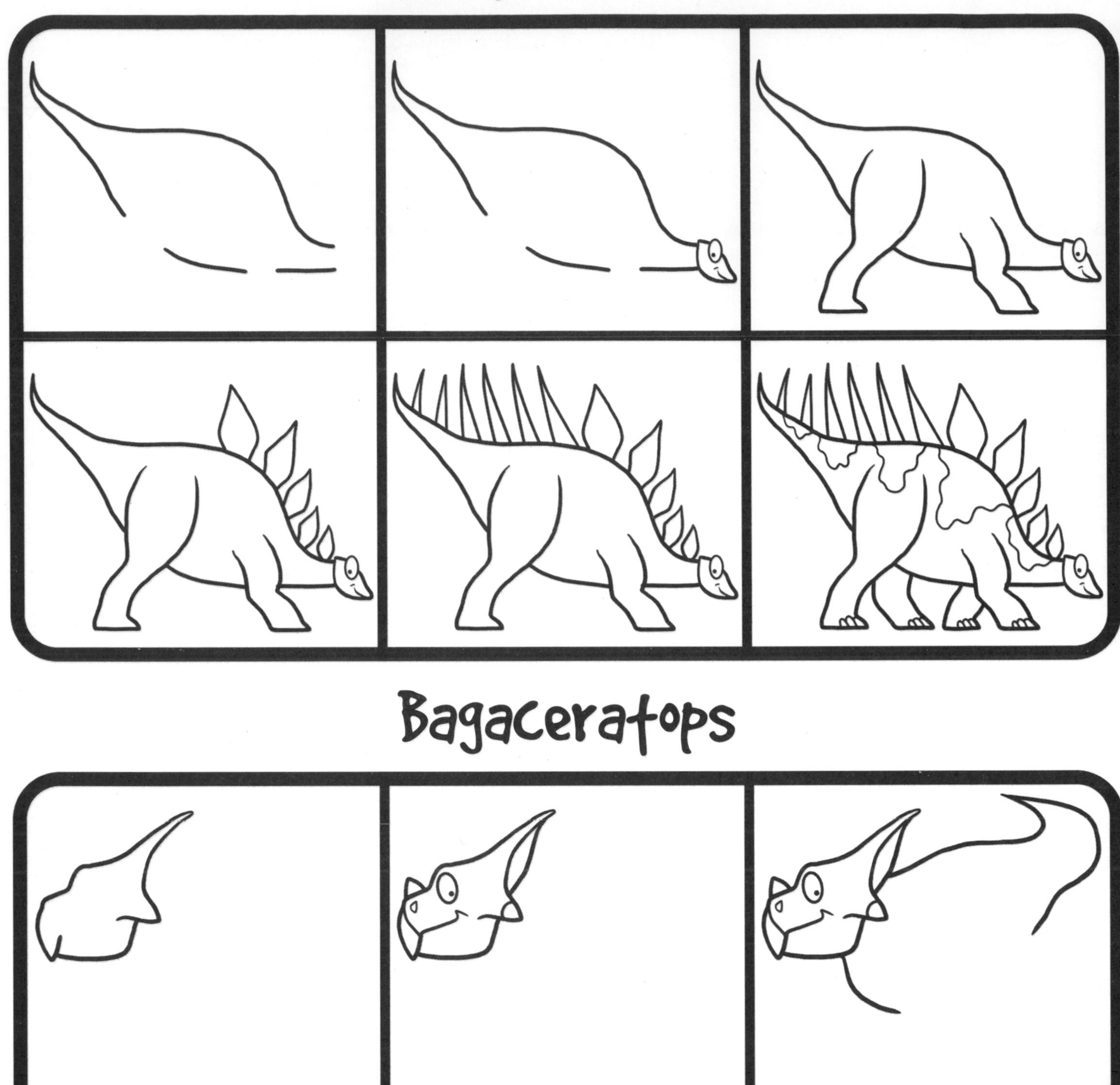

Bagaceratops

Conchoraptor

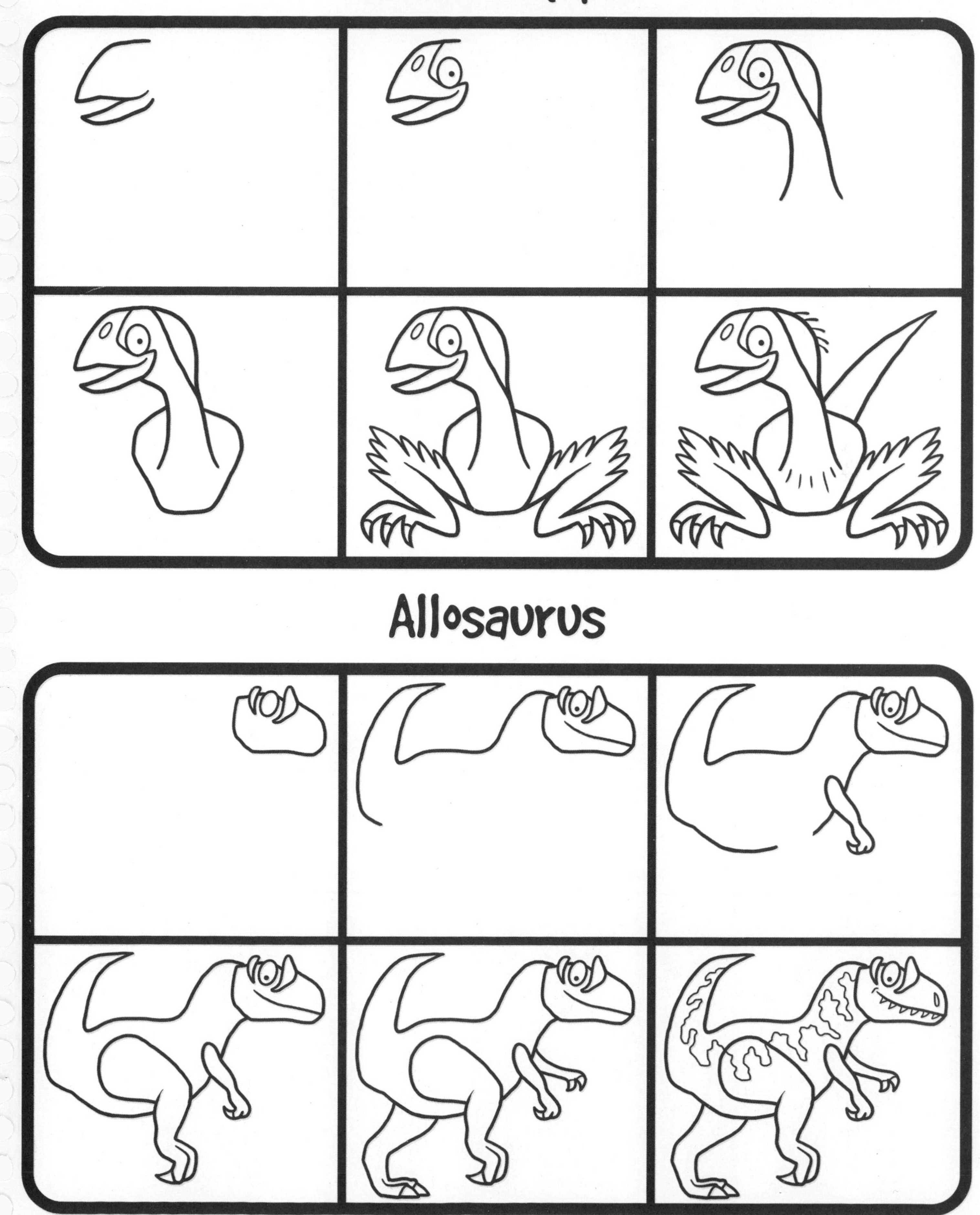

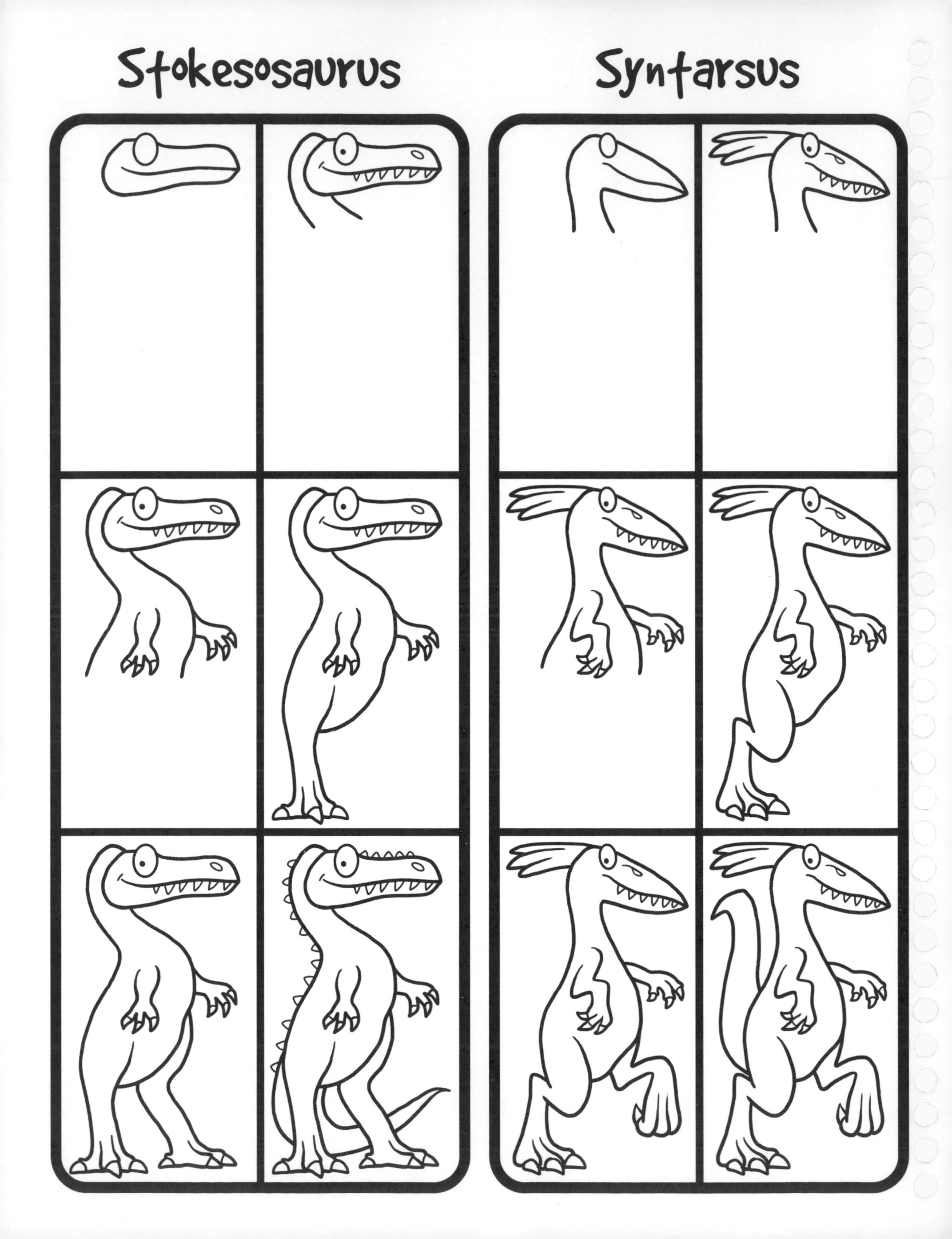
Stokesosaurus
Syntarsus

Wannanosaurus
Xiaosaurus

Rebbachisaurus

Megalosaurus

Maiasaura

oviraptor

Datousaurus

Gryposaurus

Avisaurus

Basilosaurus

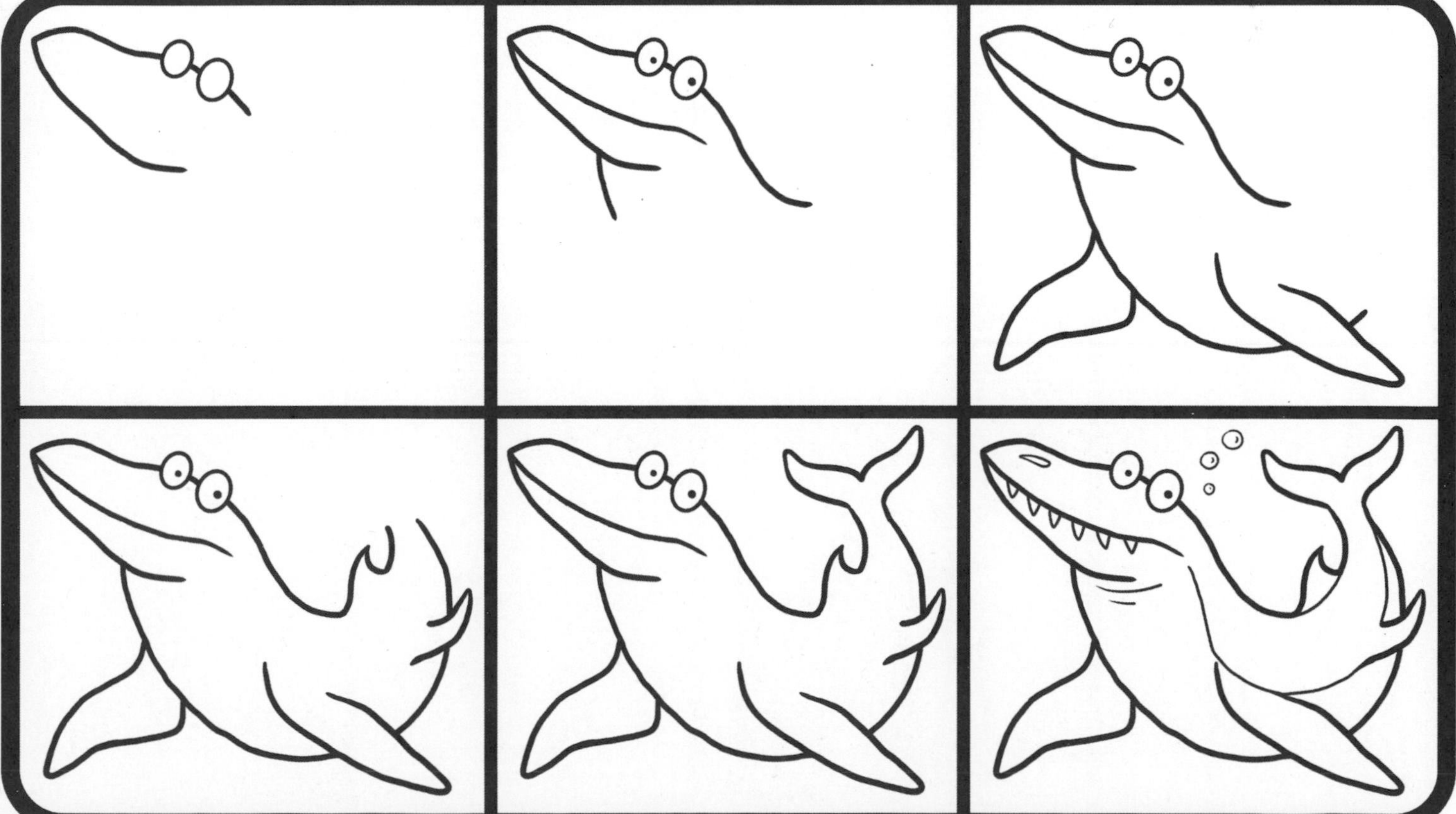

Zephyrosaurus
Rahonavis

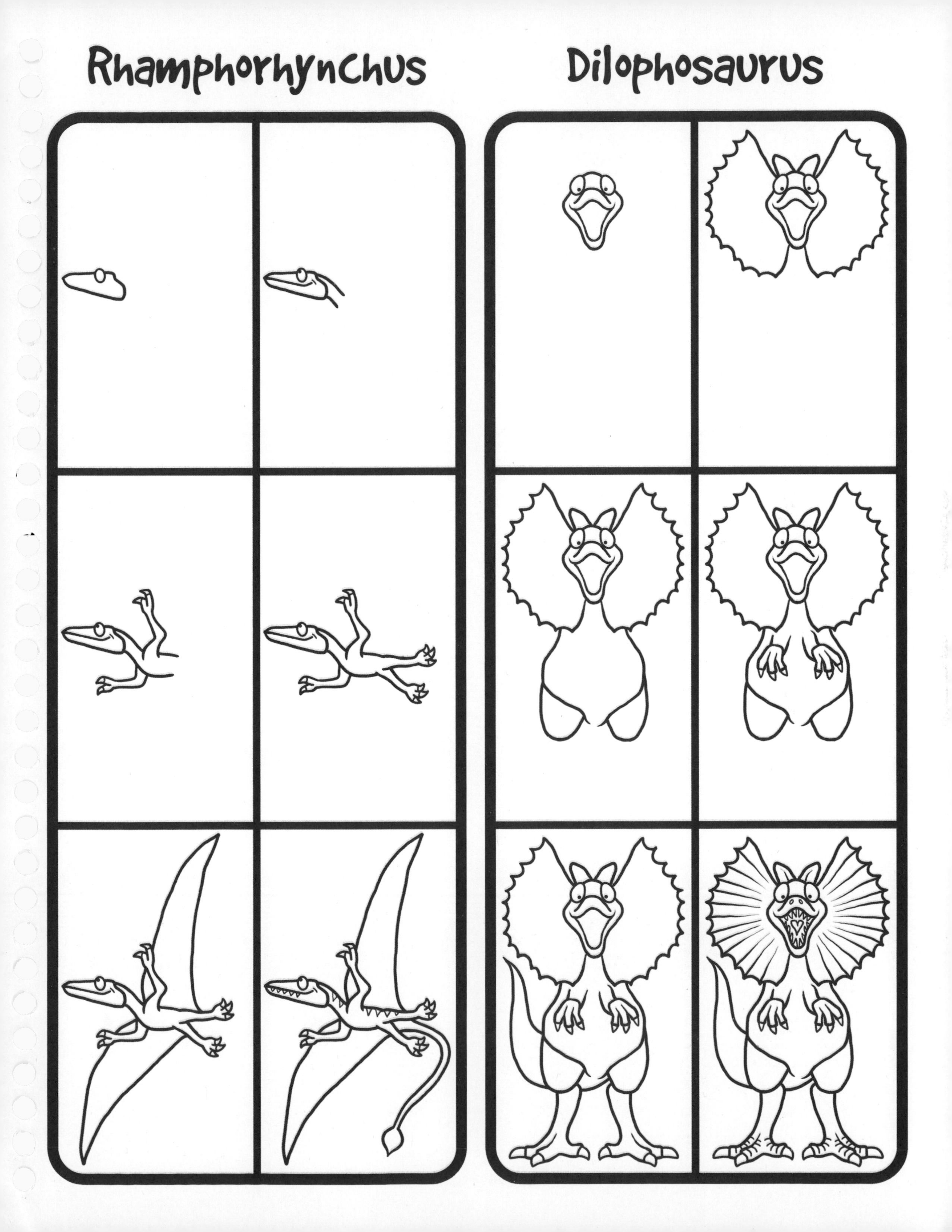
Rhamphorhynchus
Dilophosaurus

Stenopelix
Baby Dinosaur
Estemmenosuchus

Ammosaurus
Yinlong
Antarctopelta

Archaeoceratops
Isisaurus
Sinocalliopteryx

Staurikosaurus
Stegoceras
Dracorex

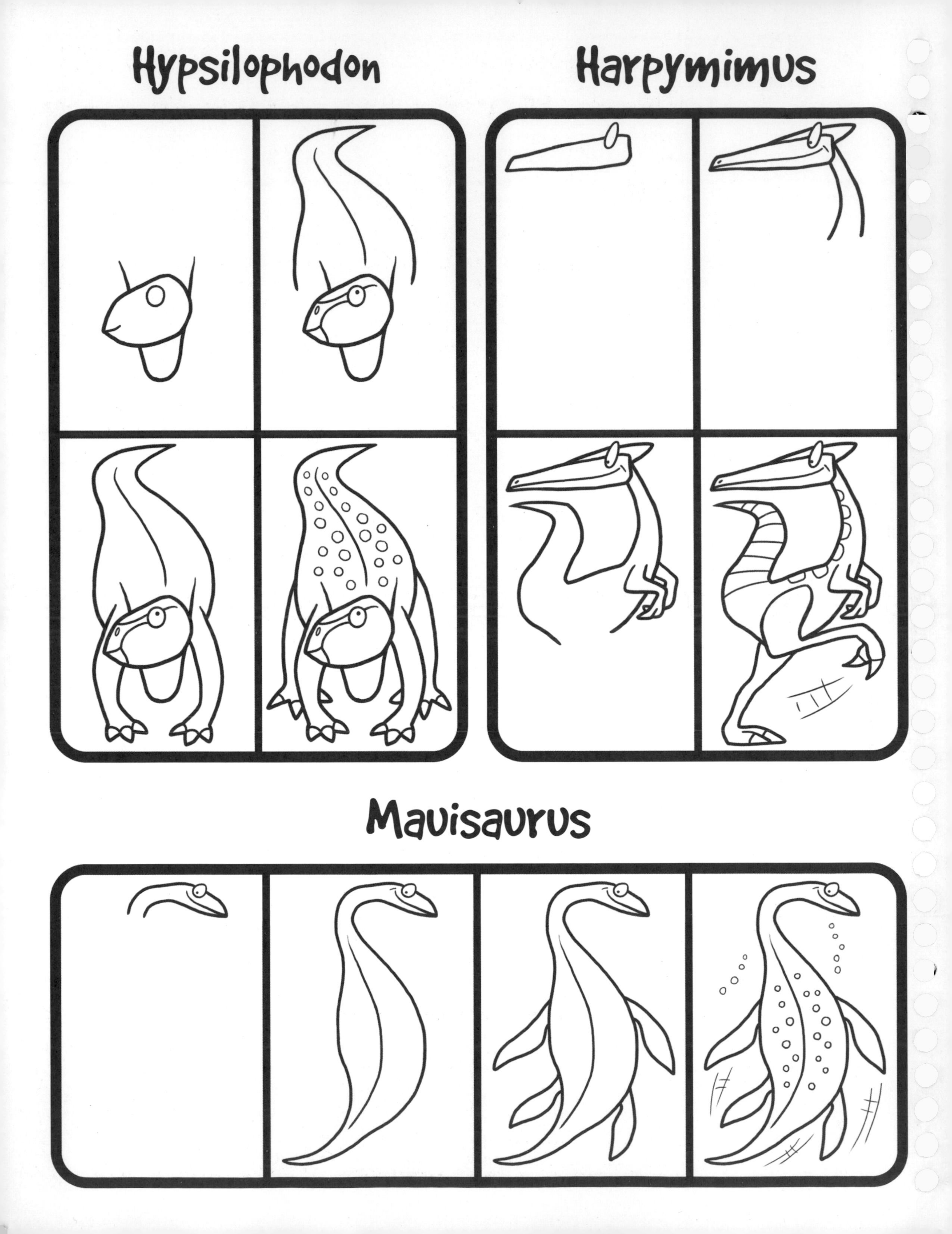
Hypsilophodon
Harpymimus
Mauisaurus